This book belongs to:

_____

_____

To my nephew Max, who would really enjoy a vacation like this one.
—O.C.

To my wife, Silvia, and our children, Corina, Antonia, and Armando.
I am only able to create my illustrations because of your support,
inspiration, and sacrifice. I love you all so very much.
—J.M.

immedium
inspiring a world of imagination

Immedium, Inc.
P.O. Box 31846
San Francisco, CA 94131
www.immedium.com

Text copyright ©2008 Oliver Chin
Illustrations copyright ©2008 Jeff Miracola

First hardcover edition published 2008.

Edited by Don Menn
Book design by Stefanie Liang

Printed in Singapore
10 9 8 7 6 5 4 3 2 1

Library of Congress Cataloging-in-Publication Data

Chin, Oliver Clyde, 1969-
  Welcome to Monster Isle / by Oliver Chin ; illustrated by Jeff Miracola. --
1st hardcover ed.
     p. cm.
  Summary: Family members whose names evoke the classic television show,
"*Gilligan's Island*," become castaways on an uncharted island, where they
encounter a menagerie of wild and colorful monsters.
  ISBN-13: 978-1-59702-016-9 (hardcover)
  ISBN-10: 1-59702-016-8
  [1. Castaways--Fiction. 2. Islands--Fiction. 3. Monsters--Fiction.] I.
Miracola, Jeff, ill. II. Title.
  PZ7.C44235We 2008
  [E]--dc22
                        2008003262

ISBN: 1-59702-016-8
ISBN 13: 978-1-59702-016-9

Welcome to Monster Isle

WRITTEN BY
OLIVER CHIN

ILLUSTRATED BY
JEFF MIRACOLA

☀ immedium · San Francisco, CA

On their vacation, the Summers family took a boat ride.
The Captain and his first mate, Tina, welcomed Mom,
Dad, Anne Marie, Finnegan, and their dog Howl.
"It's a great day for a tour," smiled Tina.
"We'll have a trip you won't forget."

However, after a few hours, the perfect weather had taken a turn for the worse.

On the horizon, the sky grew dark, the weather blustery, and the waves rough. "Let's sail home!" shouted the Captain.

But the gathering storm tossed the good ship Lollipop further out to sea. The family held on tightly as the brave crew kept them afloat. But up and down, and round and round, they spun as if in a swirling dream.

They awoke blinking at the morning sun. Fortunately, everyone was safe, but the Lollipop was strangely still. Peeking overboard onto powdery sand, Finnegan exclaimed, "We've run aground!"

Cautiously, the seven
castaways took a look
around. There were
no people, boats, or
buildings. Before them
were only a lush tropical
jungle and a monstrous
mountain looming in
the distance.

Back at the Lollipop, the Captain groaned, "The ship's hull is wrecked."

"Our charts are missing, and our radio is busted," moaned Tina.

"Are we lost?" stammered Dad.
"Marooned?" screamed Anne Marie.
"On a deserted island?" asked Mom.
"Cool!" grinned Finnegan.

Suddenly, a mammoth volcano rumbled,

krack-a-Boa!

Smoke and sounds filled the air.

YOWZA!

GOO!

WHISS!

AWK!

RAR!

FIZZ!

OOGA!

As the calls echoed around the huddled survivors, Howl whimpered nervously.

"If we split up, we might find help faster," Mom proposed.
"Afterwards, we'll meet to share what we've found."

"Lovey," Dad sighed. "We're so lucky to have
a professor in the family." He kissed her
and they split into two teams.

The Captain, Mom, Finnegan, and Howl were Team #1. With some supplies, they headed left, where a trail hugged the coast. From the tall grass, a pair of glowing eyes watched them carefully.

Dad, Tina, and Anne Marie were Team #2. They went right, where a winding path disappeared into a dark forest. But hidden in the leaves, perched a mysterious figure that cackled in anticipation.

Team #1 continued its wandering, and Finnegan noticed large footsteps leading into the thorny brush.

The wind began blowing wildly, and Howl growled at a strange shadow stretched in front of them.

Out of the bush jumped a hairy beast with huge feet! The furry Yowie yelped, YOWZA! YOWZA!

Pulling Finnegan along, the Captain ordered, "Let's go, little buddy!" Off they scampered with the Big Foot in hot pursuit.

BARK! BARK!

Team #2 inched through the jungle, and Anne Marie heard a frightful whistle.

In the branches of the highest tree was a feathered snake. It whipped its twisting tail and flashed its scales in the falling rain.

As the shower increased, the plumed Quetzalcoatl [ket-sahl-koh-AHT-l] hissed, **WHISS! WHISS!**

Hastily, Dad hollered, "Everybody exit stage right!" Swiftly, the shimmering bird slithered after them.

Leaving the Yowie out back, Team #1 felt a drumbeat shake the earth. In the clearing, an enormous bull stomped furiously. Thunder rolled through the heavens, as the creature shook its heavy mane and sharp horns.

As rain turned to sleet, the menacing mountain mumbled, "Krack-a-moa!" The kicking Catoblepas [cat-o-BLEE-puss] snorted, **RAR! RAR!**

"Let's head to greener pastures," Mom suggested, and they dashed away from the red bull.

Escaping the rain forest, Team #2 climbed uphill. Trudging through snowdrifts, the trio stopped to rest and gazed at the frozen peaks. There stood a frost giant, who hailed them with its icy breath.

Atop the boulders, the Abominable Snowman roared, **FIZZ! FIZZ!**

Fearing an avalanche, Tina whispered to her shivering teammates, "Give him the cold shoulder." So they quickly skied down the slopes.

Fleeing dangerous hooves, Team #1 came to a nearby lake. A thick fog blanketed the travelers.

But through the mist, they squinted at a giant serpent swimming towards them.

Finnegan flashed his camera
and proudly proclaimed,
"I got him!"

Skimming the waves, the
startled Ogopogo trumpeted, OOGA! OOGA!

Chased by the sea monster,
the squad scurried downstream.

Seeking shelter
from the blizzard,
Team #2 hid in a
cave. Just then
Mom realized
they had entered
someone's home.

Sporting an eagle's head
and wings on a lion's body,
the den's owner rested
upon a golden nest.

Outside, lightning split the clouds.
The surprised Gryphon unfurled its massive
wings and curved claws, and screeched, **AWK!**
AWK!

Bolting from the lair, Anne Marie
squealed, "Don't leave me behind!"

Both Teams #1 and #2 dashed back towards the beach. Everyone was glad to be reunited, but suddenly Howl barked, "Woof! Woof!" The ocean bubbled as a terrible lizard rose up, and waterfalls poured off its spiny back.

The quaking mountain grumbled, "Krack-a-zoa!" and the fiery Zillard bellowed like a hurricane, GOO! GOO!

Soon the other monsters arrived at the shore. Surprised to see each other, they nervously held their ground.

Wails resounded from every direction. "Great plan, Mom!" whined Anne Marie.

"What do we do now, dear?" begged Dad, but Finnegan wanted a closer look at the amazing animals.

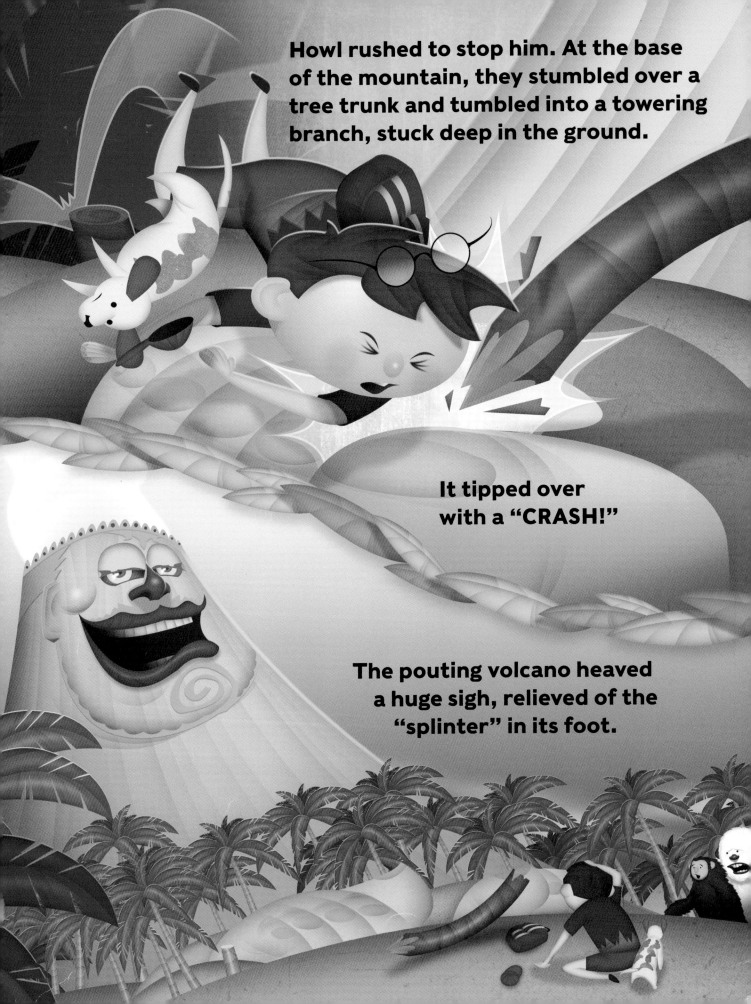

Howl rushed to stop him. At the base of the mountain, they stumbled over a tree trunk and tumbled into a towering branch, stuck deep in the ground.

It tipped over with a "CRASH!"

The pouting volcano heaved a huge sigh, relieved of the "splinter" in its foot.

The puffing monsters stopped in their tracks and faced their neighbors for the first time...in silence. With the titanic racket finally gone, the weather cleared, the sun shone, and a rainbow gently touched the island.

"All their yelling made them afraid of each other," marveled the Captain. Sure enough, the monsters weren't scary any more, especially to each other.

Finnegan predicted, "Now that everyone has met, we should all be more neighborly."

Quickly, man and beast became pals. They played, picnicked, and paraded about. Howl told his new chums what had happened to their boat, and they eagerly agreed to help them return home.

The Lollipop's crew and passengers fondly said goodbye to the island and its monsters. This time, their cries were simply of friendship. Then the people hitched a special ride across the deep blue sea.

Back at port, the explorers received a rousing welcome. Everyone asked them what had happened, where they had gone, and whom they had seen.

Now the Summers family had a vacation they'd always remember, but kept some secrets to themselves.
"That was quite a trip, Skipper," smiled Finnegan.
"When is our next visit to Monster Isle?"

OGOPOGO

Related to Scotland's Loch Ness Monster, this huge swimming serpent lives in a lake and secretly guards its territory.

GRYPHON

Sporting an eagle's speedy flight with a lion's might, this lord of the air and earth protects its golden nest from intruders.

CATOBLEPAS

Stronger than a buffalo, this beast has heavy horns and an armored back. Beware of its bloodshot gaze and short temper.

YOWIE

This legendary ape-man is covered in hair from head to big toe. Agile, alert, and always elusive, it roams The Outback.